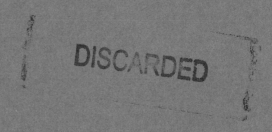

My Only Child, There's No One Like You

Dear Mama and Papa Bear:

Perhaps you have heard the myth that only children are spoiled, whiny, and selfish. Not so ... the truth of the matter is that onlies are very independent, conscientious, diligent, and dependable. In fact, if you want a job done right, hire an only child.

Onlies are little adults by age seven ... most likely to grow up to be scientists, pilots, anesthesiologists, professors, or English teachers or to succeed in other professions where perfection is rewarded.

Your only child, whether seven or seventeen, will enjoy this book. He or she will learn just how much he or she is loved and how advantageous it is to be an only child. As one only child told me when I asked why she was an only child, "Doc, I think Mom and Dad thought they reached perfection the very first try."

By the way, it might be a good idea to start looking for that youngest or middle child for your little cub to marry someday.

Blessings to you and your only child.

My Only Child, There's No One Like You

Dr. Kevin Leman
& Kevin Leman II

Illustrated by
Kevin Leman II

R Revell
Grand Rapids, Michigan

Published by Fleming H. Revell
a division of Baker Publishing Group
P.O. Box 6287, Grand Rapids, MI 49516-6287

Printed in the United States of America

Library of Congress Cataloging-in-Publication Data
Leman, Kevin
    My only child, there's no one like you / Kevin Leman & Kevin Leman II; illustrated by Kevin Leman II.
        p.   cm.
    Summary: Mama Bear shows just how special her little cub is by pointing out all of his special qualities and Only Bear knows that he is, indeed, loved.
    ISBN 0-8007-1864-X (cloth)
    [1. Only child—Fiction. 2. Family life—Fiction. 3. Bears—Fiction.] I. Leman, Kevin, II ill. II. Title.
PZ7.L537345Myd 2005
[E]—dc22
                                                                        2005009137

This book is affectionately dedicated to
Lauren Elizabeth Backus.
I can't wait to see what you do in life.
Whatever you do,
you're going to pursue it
with the excellence exemplary
of an only child.
—Dr. Kevin Leman

One day Only Cub came home from school as usual and let himself into the den. Usually Mama Bear called a hello from the kitchen. But this time Mama Bear and Papa Bear didn't hear Only Cub. They were watching the evening news.

"Oh, look at that!" Mama Bear said to Papa Bear. "The Browns had triplets in the South Forest this morning!" Mama Bear sounded excited.

Papa Bear chuckled. "Wow, are they in for some fun!"

Only Cub paused at the door, then called out, "Hello!"

"O h, cubby, I didn't hear you!" Mama said as she hurried to him. She gave Only Cub a big bear hug and moved on into the kitchen.

Only Cub followed Mama Bear. He sat at the table with his after-school snack and watched her prepare dinner.

"Mama," he said, "can I ask you something?"

"Sure, honeybear," said Mama as she chopped carrots.

was just wondering . . . well . . ." Only Cub hesitated, then blurted out, "Do you and Papa want another cub? I mean, do you need someone more to love besides me?"

Mama stopped chopping. "Oh my, my, my!" she said, and in two quick steps she scooped Only Cub up and into her arms. "No, no, no, my darling." She sank into her chair and held Only Cub close. "Where's our photo album?"

Only Cub pointed to the hutch nearby. Mama Bear reached right over and grabbed the big book and laid it on the table with a thump.

"Let me show you something special."

We knew your room
had to be special,
just like you!

"Only Cub, did you know that Papa and I waited a very long time for you?" Mama said as she opened the big book. "We wanted to be sure we were ready for the very big responsibility that comes with a very little bear."

Only Cub liked hearing stories about when he was younger. As he cuddled closer to his mama, he knew he'd like this story a lot.

Mama Bear continued. "When we knew you were on the way, Papa spent a lot of time on your room making it just the way you'd need it. Your grandma and grandpa helped too! They were almost as excited as Papa and I were when they found out you were coming."

Mama turned the page. "Let's see . . ."

Your aunt loved you
so much, you almost
couldn't breathe!

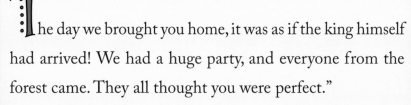he day we brought you home, it was as if the king himself had arrived! We had a huge party, and everyone from the forest came. They all thought you were perfect."

"Look at this picture, Mama!" Only Cub pointed. "Everyone at my party is so old! Where are all the other cubs?"

"Oh, cubby." Mama giggled. "You were the very first cubby bear in our family. That's what makes you oh so special! In fact, most of the bears that matter most to you are quite a bit older than you are. I think we old bears rubbed off on you at an early age."

"What do you mean?" Only Cub asked.

"Well, let's see . . ."

Your teachers were
lucky to get a cub
like you!

ook at this!" Mama said. "You liked to wear your papa's ties to school. And instead of using a notebook like the other cubs, you used a Paw Pilot."

Only Cub had to smile.

Mama went on. "Your teacher, Mrs. Racoonaroni, said you took learning seriously, and she loved having you in her class. Though she did say you were very particular about some things."

"Like what?"

"You didn't like to take off your shoes at nap time, and at snack time, you didn't like the food on your plate to touch."

"Mrs. Racoonaroni said all that?"

"Yes, and she grinned the whole time. She also pointed out how patient and reliable you were. She said you were the best line leader in kinderforest. And in geography, you knew all about every place in the animal kingdom."

"Do you know why, Mama?" Only Cub became very excited.

"Tell me!" Mama said as she turned the page.

Maps! I love maps! I know exactly where everything is when I see a map!"

"Yes, you do like to know where things are, don't you?" Mama Bear smiled. "That's probably why you like to put everything you use right back the way it should be. And you line your CDs up just so."

Only Cub nodded. "Grandpa Grizzly says they last longer if you do that."

Mama laughed. "That's true! Do you know what I like about you?"

"What, Mama?"

"Let's see . . ."

We'd be lost
without you on our
family vacations.

The day you found Flash was a
great day for both of you.

I like how you take care of your pet turtle, Flash. I like how his water dish is always fresh and nearly full. You're very patient with Flash. You know, turtles are known for their patience too. Maybe that's why you two get along so well."

"I love Flash," said Only Cub. "I knew I wanted him right when I saw him."

"Oh, honeybear, you usually know exactly what you want, that's true, and Papa and I find it hard to sway your mind from it. Although you can be a little stubborn sometimes, you're also very responsible and so caring to all the animals in the forest and to your papa and me.

"Papa and I pour a lot of love and time into you, but it could never measure up to how much you give back to us."

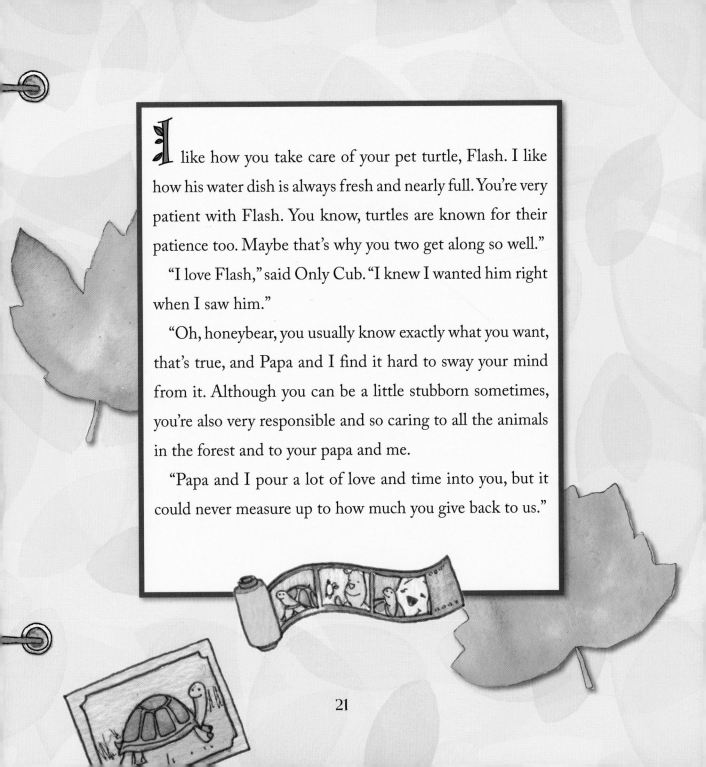

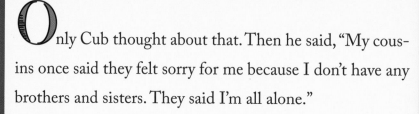

Only Cub thought about that. Then he said, "My cousins once said they felt sorry for me because I don't have any brothers and sisters. They said I'm all alone."

Mama looked at her cub. "The thing is, you play so well alone. You have an amazing imagination that takes you wherever you'd like to go! That's why you and your papa play so well together. He has as much fun with you as you do with him!"

Mama Bear pointed to a picture. "Who's this, honey?"

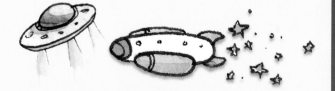

You have an "out of this world" imagination!

Your first
yearbook picture.

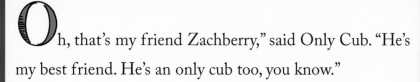

Oh, that's my friend Zachberry," said Only Cub. "He's my best friend. He's an only cub too, you know."

Mama peered closer. "I must admit that Papa and I worried a little about having an only cub. We knew you liked to play with other cubs, so we put you in situations where you could play with your cousins and school buddies." She folded her paws. "And you thrived so well. Papa and I don't worry about you anymore. You're going to be a fine grown-up bear in the forest someday."

Mama glanced at the clock on the wall. "Oh dear! I'd better put these pictures away and finish making dinner."

The bears ate a scrumptious meal. Afterward, Papa Bear leaned back and patted his belly. He roared a big yawn and winked at Only Cub. "I think I'll go sleep this off," he said, and he headed out of the kitchen.

Mama Bear moved to the stove. "Cubby, would you like another plate of honey-bunny pot roast?"

"Oh, no thank you, Mama," Only Cub said. "One plate was just perfect!"

"One plate? Are you sure you don't need *three*?"

"I'm sure." And then Only Cub realized what his mama was saying. "Sometimes one is all you need!"

"See?" Mama beamed. "That's exactly what I mean!"

ama Bear sat back down next to her cub and placed her paw over Only Cub's paw. "I am so proud of you, my one and only cub. You're all I need. Don't ever forget, I love you very much and always will. We'll always be a part of each other, and no matter where you go, you'll always live in my heart. And I want you to know something else.

"There's no one like you."

Only Cub knew Mama and Papa
Bear loved him and that their little
family would always be close.
And they always were.

A book for every cub in the forest

Dr. Kevin Leman & Kevin Leman II

My Youngest, There's No One Like You

Illustrated by Kevin Leman II

Dr. Kevin Leman & Kevin Leman II

My Firstborn, There's No One Like You

Illustrated by Kevin Leman II

Dr. Kevin Leman & Kevin Leman II

My Middle Child, There's No One Like You

Illustrated by Kevin Leman II